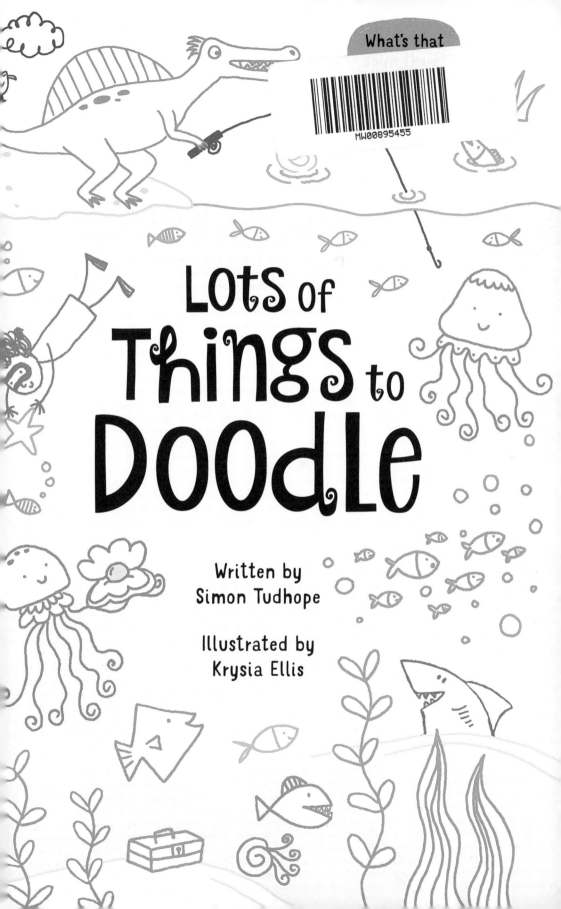

LOTS of THINGS to DOODLE

Written by
Simon Tudhope

Illustrated by
Krysia Ellis

Contents

Hello!

Use your pens or pencils to complete the doodle on each page.

Add faces, patterns and other details.

Fill the spaces with anything you like!

DOODLING
Animals

Let's get going!

Meoww

Who's going to win the prize for the LONGEST tentacles?

7

These zebras
have AMAZING
patterns.

Check out
my mane!

My pattern is
much better
than stripes!

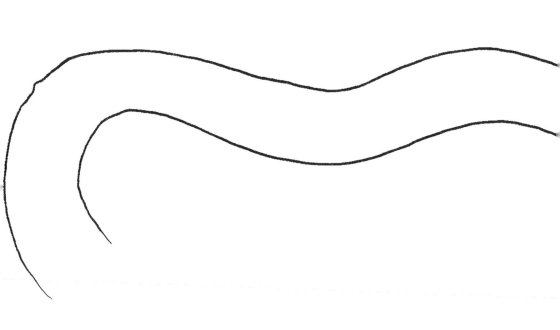

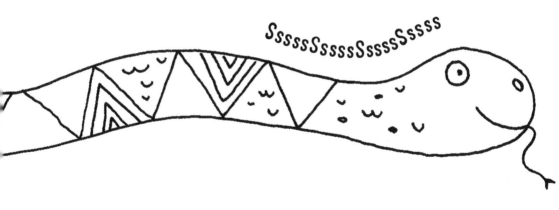

SsssSssssSssssSsss

THE EARLY BIRD
COSTUME PARTY

Your coat's VERY
stylish, Nellie.

My hairstyle is best!

ALPACA

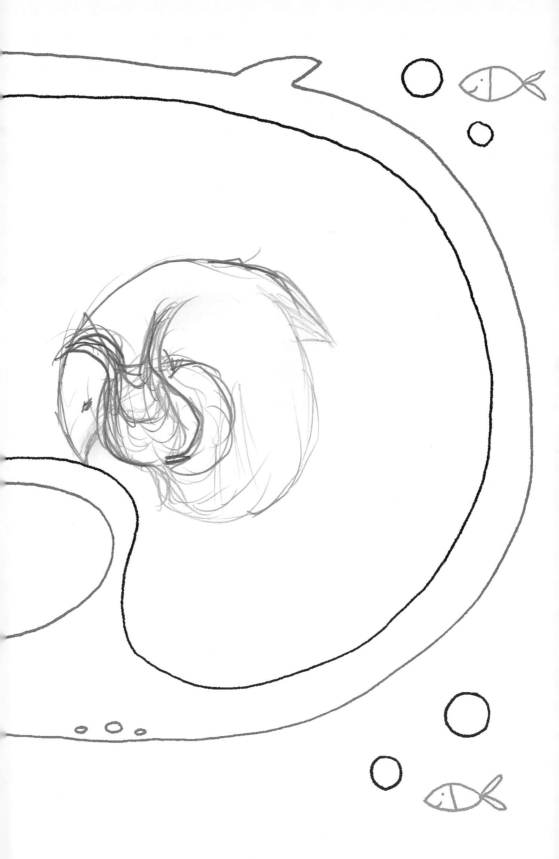

FINGERPRINT ANIMALS

DOODLING
People

Drawing is FUN!

Who's fallen off their board?

AGH!

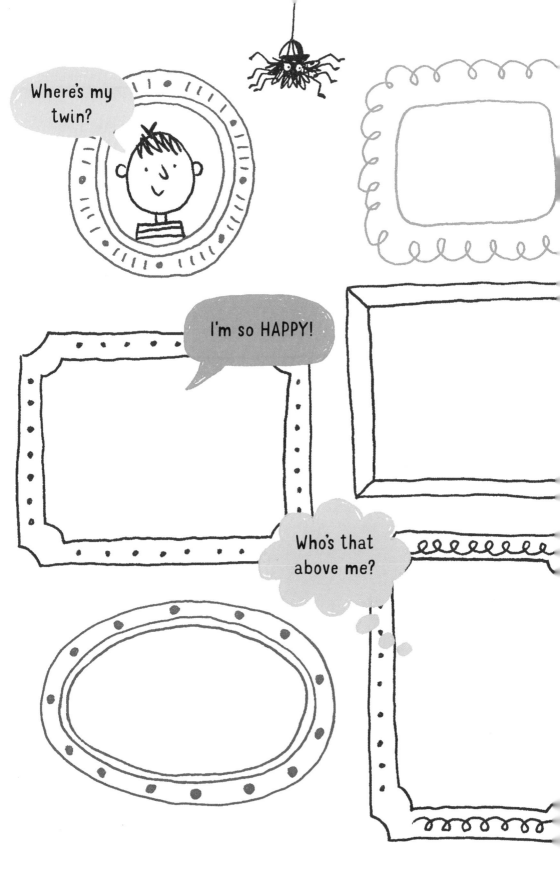

42

And he's **BIGGER** than me!

And I'm **BIGGEST** of all!

Uh-ohhhh...

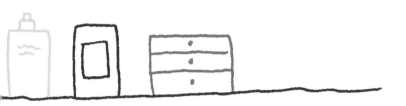

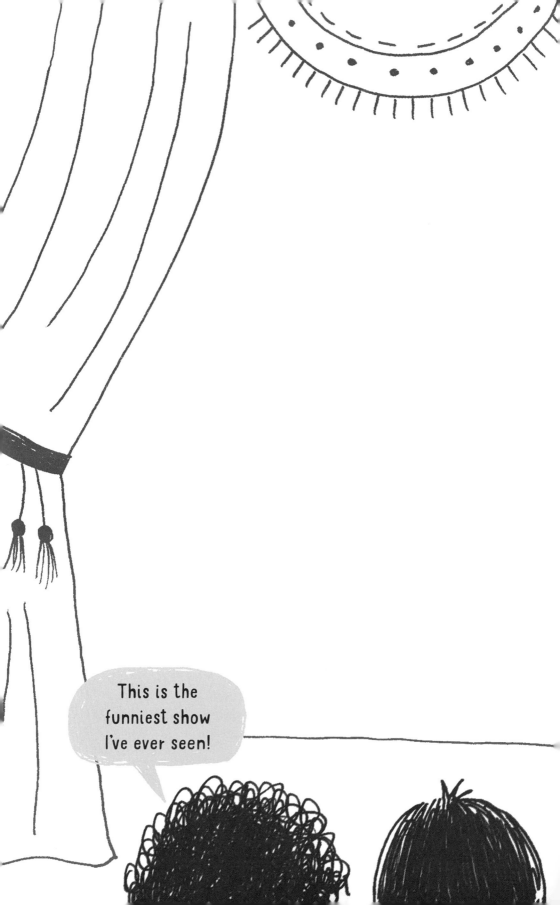

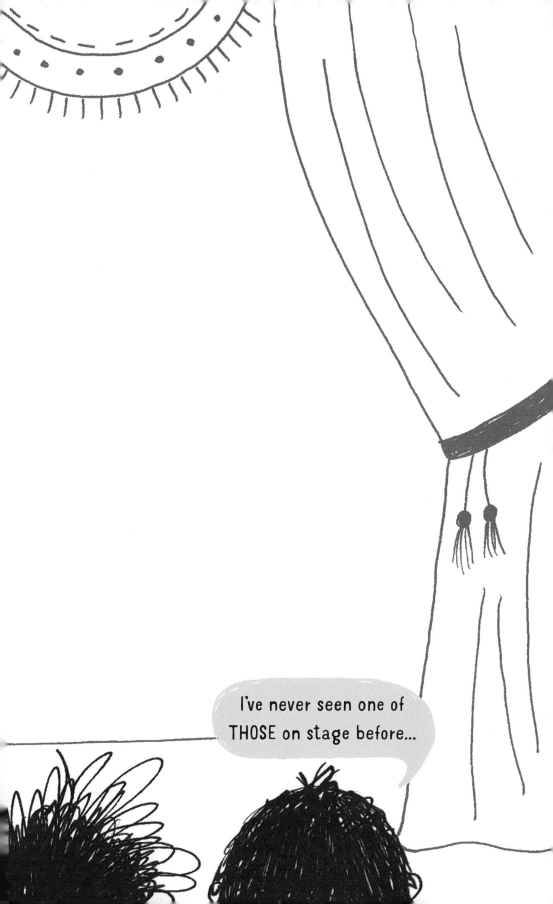

What's in that old chest?

I think there's something hiding in the shipwreck...

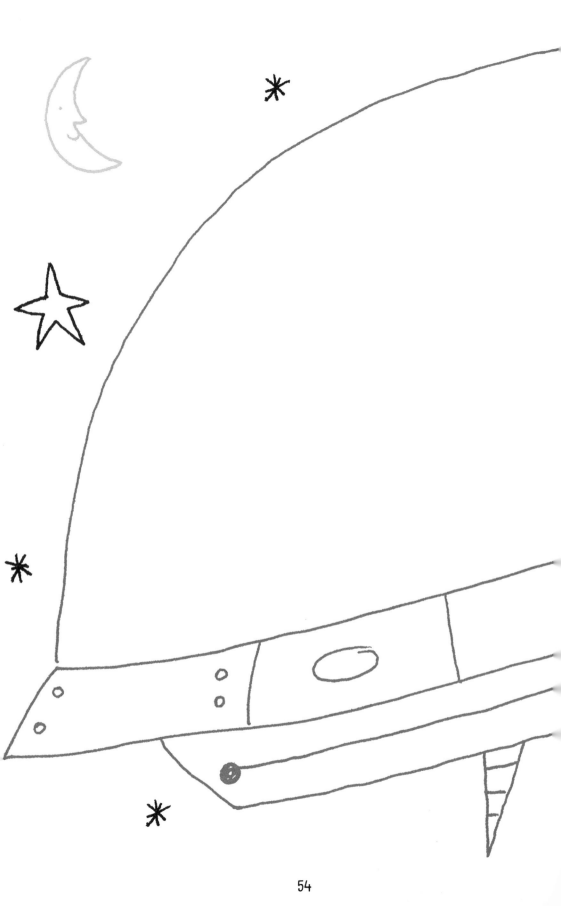

58

How are all these other people feeling?

63

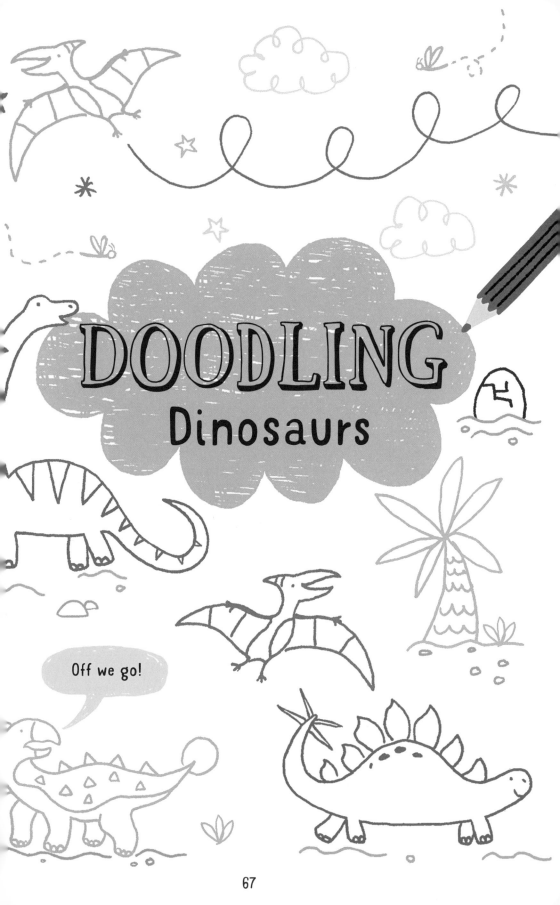

DOODLING
Dinosaurs

Off we go!

I've got the
LONGEST
NECK.

I'm the
SPIKIEST!

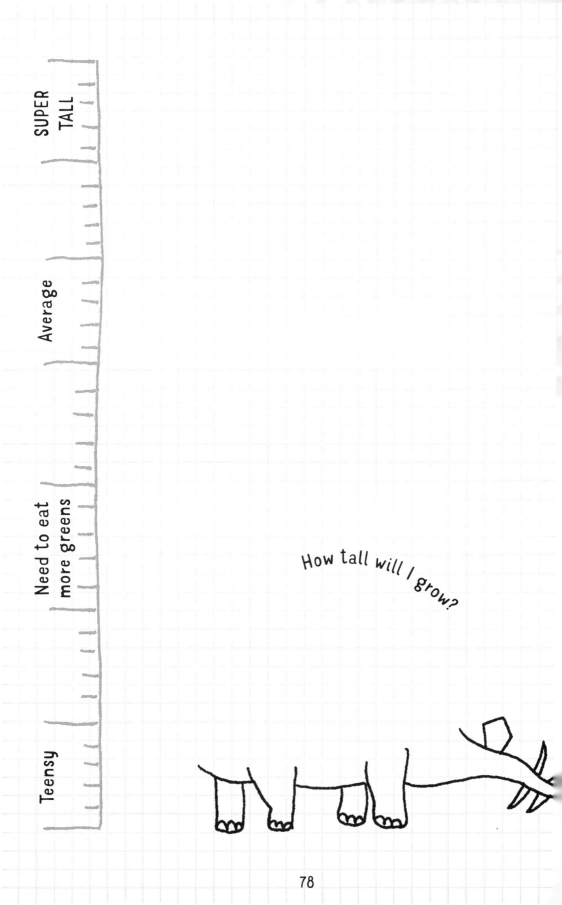

SUPER TALL

Average

Need to eat
more greens

Teensy

How tall will I grow?

How about me?

And me?

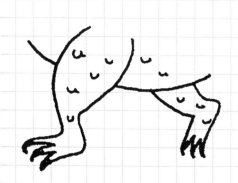

DRIED
LEAVES

Family day out

y faces

First day at school

WORLD **CHAMPION** DINOSAUR

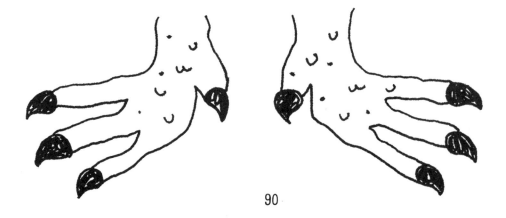

SCREEECH! It's erupting!

LET'S GET OUT OF HERE!

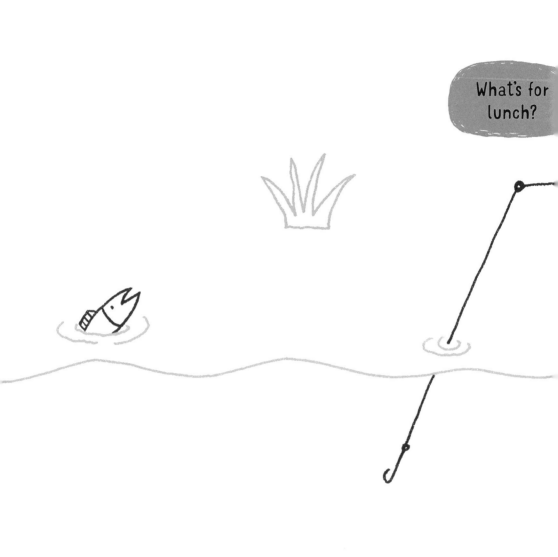

What's for lunch?

94

DOODLING
Things that go

Beep beeep!

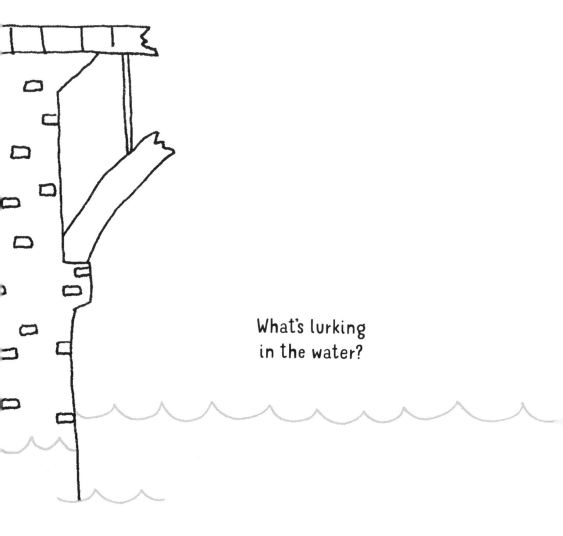

What's lurking
in the water?

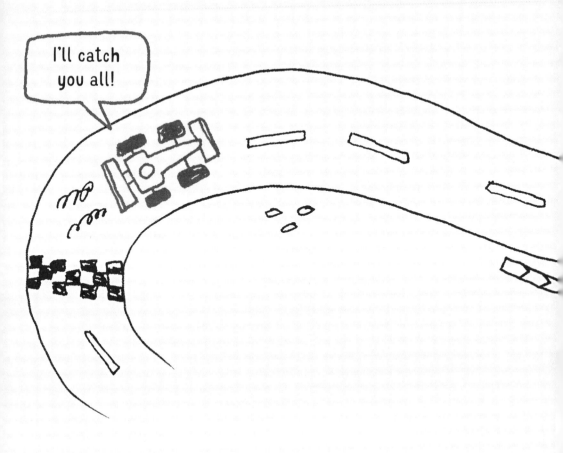

Quick - finish the track so the cars can complete the race.

ARGH!

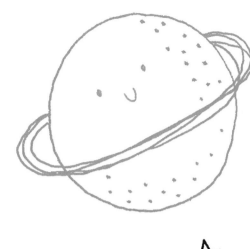

What's that in the sky?

And what's THAT
on the mountain?!

BEEEEEEP!

119

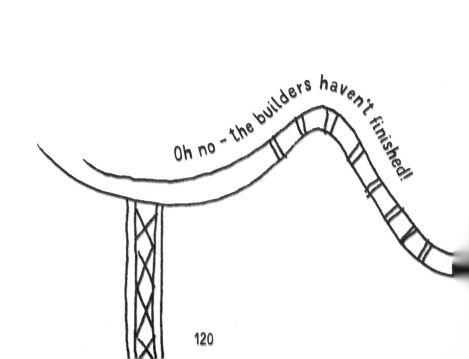

Oh no – the builders haven't finished!

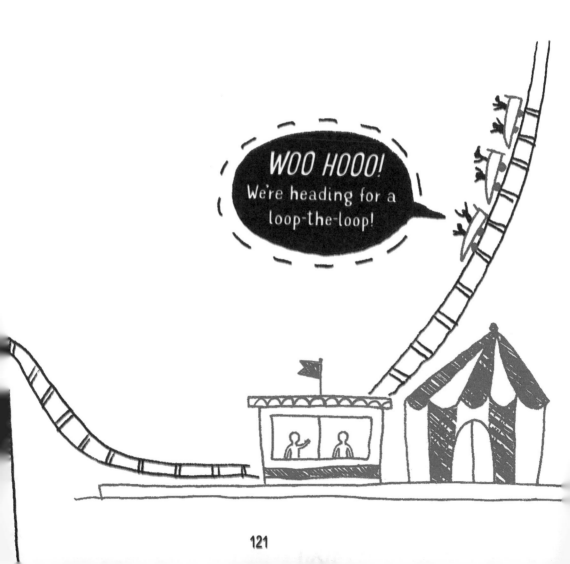

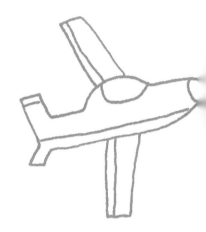